THE FOURTH of VIRGIL'S ÆNEID, and THE NINTH BOOK of VOLTAIRE'S HENRIAD

Translated by Anonymous

TO MONSIEUR DELILLE.

SIR,

After reading with infinite pleasure your masterly translations of Virgil, I have been led into a train of reflection on the mechanism of words, and on the manners, the ideas, and pursuits of Nations in as much as they frequently give rise to the difference of character which we remark in their language. Few literary discussions would I think be more curious than an impartial comparative enquiry of this kind.

Not only have the easy elegance and courtly air of your verses displayed the French tongue in these respects worthy of your original; but have inclined me to think that they have raised it near the highest pitch of perfection of which it is at present capable, in the translation of a Latin poet. After two brillant ages of literature the French language did not, till you appeared, possess one translation of the great masterpieces of antiquity, which might fairly be said to have attained the rank of a classical work: while the English had been long enriched with such translations of most of them, as will like yours, in all probability share the immortality of their originals. In the cloud of critics which superior lustre necessarily attracts, many perhaps were not sufficiently aware of the peculiar difficulties of your undertaking, from the nature of the materials which you had to employ, and some not candid enough to compare the work which you have raised out of them, with what they had hitherto been made to produce.

That the English language might be so managed as to surpass the French in expression of strong sentiments, in boldness of imagery, in harmony and variety of versification I will not be sufficiently hardy to assert. The universality of the latter must be admitted as a strong presumption of its general excellency. Yet I cannot help wishing, that some pen worthy to be compared with Monsieur Delille's would give the world an opportunity of judging whether the former may not have some pretensions to superiority in the instances which I have mentioned.

Besides the length of time which has elapsed since the production of Dryden's translation, you will recollect with a sigh, as I do, his own expression: «What Virgil wrote in the vigor of age, in plenty and at ease, I have undertaken to translate,» says Dryden, «in my declining years, struggling with want, oppressed with sickness, curbed in my genius, liable to be misunderstood in all I write.—What I now offer is the wretched remainder of a sickly age, worn out by study and oppressed by Fortune»!

It might not therefore be deemed sufficient to compare a work, produced under such disadvantages, in the seventeenth century, (notwithstanding the extraordinary powers of its author) with what is now becoming the admiration of the nineteenth. Much less, sir, will it be just or candid to suppose me capable of publishing my feeble attempt with any view of comparison as to the merit of the performance.—Should it be asked, what then could have been my inducement?—First, if I am fortunate enough to excite others more capable than myself to try again the comparative force of English language in a new translation, as you have just shown how much can be done in French, I shall have obtained the utmost bounds of my ambition.

Secondly, I am happy to acknowledge the pleasure which I felt an employing some long moments of leisure, on a subject wherein your genius had taken such delight: I hove chosen the fourth book as that which I have had the good fortune of hearing in your own verses, with all the charms of your own recitation; and have pursued this occupation.

Non ita certandi cupidus, quam propter amorem
Quod te imitari aveo——

I have the honor to be with great respect,
Your most obedient humble servant,

P. L.

PREFACE.

The motives and design of this attempt are sufficiently explained in the foregoing address, the ideas which gave rise to it have been confirmed and enlarged in its progress. As some apology for them, it may not be improper to observe here, that the English language seems to owe a great portion of that energy for which it is remarked, to the old Anglo Saxon idiom, which still forms its basis. It was enriched and softened by the introduction of the French, though some are of opinion that most of its foreign words, were adopted immediately from the Latin and not from any modern tongue: and this opinion is corroborated by the observation, that, during more than a century after the conquest, very little mixture of French is perceivable in the style of English authors. Be that as it may, it is certain that the constant attention of its earliest writers to the Greek and Latin models, though sometimes carried to excess, has added grace, variety, and extent to its construction. Sir Thomas Brown who wrote his *Pseudodoxia Epidemica*, or Enquiry into Vulgar Errors, about the middle of the seventeenth century, and whose style is still much commended, says in his preface to that interesting work: «I confess that the quality of the subject, will sometimes carry us into expressions beyond meer English apprehensions. And indeed if elegancy of style proceedeth, and English pens maintain that stream we have of late observed to flow from many, we shall, in a few years, be fain to learn Latin to understand English, and a work will prove of equal facility in either». Milton, both in his verse and prose, has carried this affectation to such a degree, as not only to be frequently beyond a meer English apprehension, but even beyond that of an ordinary proficient in the learned languages. Yet, so far were these innovations from being considered as prejudicial, that one of the most admired writers of our days, Dr. Johnson, did not scruple to confess, that he formed his style upon the model of Sir Thomas Brown. The great number of excellent translations which were constantly appearing through all its progressive stages of improvement, must naturally have given the language a classical turn. It is scarcely possible that a work so extensive, and so universally read, as Pope's admirable translation of Homer, should not leave some gloss of grecism upon the idiom into which so many of its greatest beauties had been transfused. At the same time the early and proud independence of the middle orders of people in England, prevented them from conforming their language, their manners, or their sentiments to the model of a court. Whereby if their expression did not acquire politeness from that quarter, it did not loose any of its strength. While the energy which their language is allowed to possess is the old inheritance of their Anglo Saxon ancestors, whatever elegance it may have acquired, is derived rather from Athens and Rome than from St. James's.—The varied and extended occupations of a maritime and commercial people have increased the fund from which imagery in discourse is drawn, and as all occupations in such a nation are deemed honorable, no metaphor is rejected as ignoble that is apt and expressive.

A number of ideas conveyed by monosyllables gives great force and conciseness, but leaves the poet frequently to struggle with the harshness of sound; nevertheless those who are conversant with English poetry will have perceived that this difficulty is not always insuperable. The different accentuation of the old Anglo Saxon words, with those adopted from other tongues, affords uncommon variety and emphasis to the numbers of English verse. The measure commonly used in poetry of a higher style is of ten syllables, as that in French is of twelve. Three English verses of ten syllables generally contain nearly the same number of syllables as two Latin or Greek hexameters, but are in most instances capable of conveying more ideas, especially in translating from Greek which abounds so much in what seem to us expletive particles. The *cæsura*, or pause is not invariably fixed on the same syllable of the verse, as in French; in the choice and variety of its position, consists the chief art of appropriate harmony. Accentuation of syllables, which seems, to answer the idea of long and short syllables in the dead languages, is the foundation of English, metre.—Tripple rhymes used with judgment have been admitted by the best English poets, and now and then the introduction of an Alexandrine, or verse of six feet.

Though blank verse has still many admirers, the English ear is grown remarkably delicate as to the consonance of rhymes; Dryden and Pope have used many, which would not now be received. Masculine and feminine rhymes are unknown in English. As the character of a language appears to be the result of all the affections of the people who speak it, it did not seem foreign to this design to compare the manner in which two such great genius's as Virgil and Voltaire, have treated the same subject, and to place the loves of Henry and Gabrielle in comparison with those of Æneas and Dido. The elegance, the delicacies, the nicest touches of refined gallantry come admirably forward with the brillant colouring, the light and graceful pencil of Voltaire. The verse seems to flow from his pen without effort into its natural channel, and some of his descriptions would not loose by a comparison; but perhaps he has let it be seen, that it would not be so easy a task to convey in the same language the exquisite and deep strokes of passion, which the Roman master has left to the admiration of the universe. To which of these styles the English and the French languages are most fitted, and how far they may be made to succeed in both, is one of the objects of an inquiry which this undertaking was intended to promote.

Whatever can be said by way of comment on the fourth book of the Æneid has been so often repeated, and is so easily to be met with, that it was thought needless to add any notes to this new translation. The few instances in which there may appear some difference in the interpretation of the original are scarce worth noticing. One perhaps may appear to require some apology; most of the translators of Virgil have represented Dido under the most violent impression of rage in her first speech to Æneas. Whereas it would seem that the situation of her mind is meant to be described before she addresses him, rather as wild and frantic with doubt and fear, than actuated by rage. Whatever anger she may feel, is yet so much tempered by love and hope, that she breaks out, not into the language of rage, but of the most tender expostulation, the most lively interest in his own welfare, the most pathetic painting of her feelings and situation. It is a beautiful appeal to love, to honor, and to pity. Not till after his cold answer, does she burst into all the violence of rage, of contempt, and of despair. This gradation has often been remarked as a principal beauty. As some excuse for the coldness of Æneas which takes away so much of the interest of the poem, Virgil is careful to recoil continually to our attention, that he is acting under the impulse of the divinity. Such has been the constant practice of the ancients to prevent our disgust, for the action which they represent. In Orestes and Phoedra it is the excuse of the violence of passion, in Æneas of that coldness which we find it so difficult to forgive, but which in this point of view we shall be inclined to pity.

While these sheets were in the press MONSIEUR DELILLE has given the world another proof of the powers of his mind, and displayed the French language to vast advantage, in a more arduous strain of poetry that it had yet attempted. The perspicuity for which it has always been remarked, and to which it owes its charms in conversation as perhaps also the dificulty with which it is adapted to works of poetical imagination, is strongly exemplified in his translation of Paradise Lost. If he has not always been able to make the french idiom bear him through the ætherial regions in which the daring wing of Milton's muse soars with so sublime a flight, he has descended not without dignity to the sphere of human understanding. And I believe it may be safely advanced, that it will be easier for ordinary capacities, even among English readers, to understand the work of Milton, in this translation than in the original.

* * * * *

ARGUMENT.

Æneas, after escaping from the destruction of Troy and a long series of adventures by sea and land, is driven by a storm raised by the hatred of Juno on the coast of Affrica, where he is received by Dido, in the new town of Carthage, which she was building, after her flight from the cruelty of her brother in law Pigmalion, who had murdered her husband Sicheus.—Venus dreading for her son Æneas, the influence of Juno upon the mind of Dido, makes Cupid assume the forme of his child Julus or Ascanius, and raise in the bosom of the Queen the most ungovernable passion for Æneas. The fourth book begins by Dido's confessing her weakness to her sister Anna, who gives her many plausible reasons for indulging it, and advices her to make her peace with heaven and marry her lover. Juno, finding herself outwitted by Venus and her favourite Dido irrecoverably in love, accosts Venus first in a sarcastic tone but afterwards in very persuasive language, endeavours in her turn to deceive her, by obtaining her content to the marriage, by which means to frustrate the fates which promised the empire of the world to the descendants of Æneas in Italy. Venus, aware of the deceit, appears in a very complimentary style to give into it, and consents to her projects. While the Tyrian princess and the Trojan are hunting in a forest Juno sends down a violent storm, and the Queen and Æneas take shelter alone in a dark cavern.—There Juno performed the nuptial rite and the passion of Dido was reconciled to her conscience.—Fame soon spreads the report of this alliance.—Iarba, one of Dido's suitors, hears of it and addresses an angry prayer to Jupiter Ammon from whom he was descended. Jove sends down Mercury to order Æneas to leave Carthage. Dido endeavours to make him alter this terrible resolution, falls into the most violent paroxism of rage at his cold refusal, again melts into tenderness, employs her sister to prevail upon Æneas, at least, to wait till the wintry storms were past. All is in vain, and Dido resolved to die, deceives her sister with an idea of magic rites to get rid of her passion—and persuades her to raise a funeral pyle in her palace, Æneas a second time admonished by Mercury sets sail; when Dido, at the break of day, beholds his vessels out of reach she again bursts into a violent fit of passion, but soon sinks into despair.—Accuses her sister's fatal kindness, upbraids herself with her infidelity to the memory of Sicheus, vents the most dreadful imprecations against Æneas and the Romans, who were to be his ascendants, bequeaths all her hatred to her subjects, than relaxes into a momentary tenderness at the sight of the nuptial bed, the cloaths and pictures of Æneas which she had placed on the funeral pyre, and at last puts an end to her life with the sword of her faithless lover.

THE FOURTH BOOK OF VIRGIL'S ÆNEID, TRANSLATED INTO ENGLISH VERSE.

While Dido, now with rising cares opprest,
Indulg'd the pain; the flame within her breast
In silence prey'd, and burn'd in every vein.
Fix'd in her heart, his voice, his form remain;
5 Still would her thought the Hero's fame retrace,
Her fancy feed upon his heav'nly race:
Care to her wearied frame gives no repose,
Her anxious night no balmy slumber knows;
And scarce the morn, in purple beams array'd,
10 Chas'd from the humid pole the ling'ring shade,
Her sister, fond companion of her thought,
Thus in the anguish of her soul she sought.
Dear Anna, tell me, why this broken rest?
What mean these boding thoughts? who is this guest,
15 This lovely stranger that adorns our court?
How great his mein! and what a godlike port!
It must be true, no idle voice of Fame,
From heav'n, I'm sure, such forms, such virtue came.
} Degenerate spirits are by fear betray'd,
20 } His soul, alas, what fortunes have essay'd;
} What feats of war!—and in what words convey'd!
Were it not fix'd, determin'd in my mind,
That me no more the nuptial tye shall bind,
Since Death deceiv'd the first fond flame I knew:
25 Were Hymen's rites less odious to my view,
To this one fault perhaps I might give way;
For must I own it? Anna since the day
Sicheus fell, (that day a brother's guilt,
A brother's blood upon our altars spilt);
30 He, none but he, my feelings could awake,
Or with one doubt my wav'ring bosom shake.
Yes! these are symptoms of my former flame;
But sooner thro' her very inmost frame,
May gaping Earth my sinking feet betray;
35 Jove's light'ning blast me from this vital ray
To Hell's pale shade, and Night's eternal reign,
Ere, sacred Honor, I thy rite profane.
Oh, no! to whom my virgin faith I gave,
"Twas his, and his remains within the grave".

40 She ceas'd—but down her bosom gush'd her tears.
"O dearer than the genial ray that cheers",
Her sister cry'd, shall lonely grief consume,
Lost to the joys of love your beauties bloom,
Lost to the joys, maternal feelings share?
45 Do shades for this, do buried ashes care?
That new in grief no lover should succeed,
Tyrians in vain, in vain Iarba plead;
That every chief of Afric's wide domain,
In triumphs proud, should learn to sue in vain;
50 'Twas well; but why a mutual flame withstand?
Can you forget who owns this hostile land?
Unconquer'd Getulans your walls surround,
The Syri untam'd, the wild Numidian bound.
Thro' the wide desert fierce Barceans roam:
55 Why need I mention from our former home,
The deadly war, a brother's threats prepare?
For me, I think, that Juno's fost'ring care,
Some god auspicious, rais'd the winds that bore
Those Phrygian vessels to our Lybian shore.
60 Their godlike chief should happy Dido wed,
How would her walls ascend, her empire spread?
Join'd by the arms of Troy, with such allies,
Think to what height will Punic glory rise.
Win but the gods, their sacred off'rings pay;
65 Detain your guest; invent some fond delay.
See low'ring tempests o'er the ocean ply,
The shatter'd vessels, the inclement sky».

Each word that dropt inflam'd her burning mind,
And all her wav'ring soul to love inclin'd;
70 New gleams of hope in Dido's bosom play,
And Honor's bright idea fades away.

Fain would the sisters now, by gift and pray'r,
With heav'n seduc'd, the conscious error share.
At ev'ry shrine, the fav'ring gods to gain,
75 In order due are proper victims slain;
To Ceres, Bacchus, and the God of Light,
And Juno most, who tends the nuptial rite.
Herself the goblet lovely Dido bears,
Her graceful arm the sacred vessel rears;
80 And where the horns above the forehead join,
Upon the snow-white heifer pours the wine:
Before the god with awful grace she bows,
Moves round the altar rich with daily vows,

Hangs o'er the victim, in its bosom pries,
85 And through the breathing entrail darts her eyes.
Vain cares, alas! and rites too fondly paid!
The tortur'd soul, can vows, can altars aid?
Weak boast of priests, and ineffectual pray'rs!
In her own heart, unknown, her fate she bears.
90 The pleasing flame upon her vitals feeds,
The silent wound within her bosom bleeds.
She raves, she burns, and with uncertain mind,
Roams o'er the town; roams like the wounded hind,
Whom in the woods, unconscious of his deed,
95 The hunter pierc'd, and left the trembling reed;
O'er woods, o'er quaries, from the pain she springs,
While in her flank the deadly arrow clings.
} So with Æneas love-sick Dido strays,
100 } Points to her town, her Tyrian wealth displays,
} While ev'ry look her longing soul betrays;
And fain her lips would tell the fond desire,
But scarce begun—the trembling words expire:
—When later hours convivial pleasure bring,
Then back to Troy, her thoughts impatient spring,
105 The well known story still enchants her ears,
She hangs enamour'd on each word she hears:
But when the moon with paler splendor glows,
When stars descending counsel sweet repose,
In the deserted hall, alone she mourns;
110 Each word, each look, upon her soul returns,
She sees him absent, hears him o'er again,
Presses the happy couch where he had lain;
Or with the father's rising form beguil'd,
Deludes her flame, and clasps the lovely child.
115 Each other care her burning thoughts refuse,
In arms no more her Tyrian youth she views;
No spreading moles the boistrous tide command;
The tow'rs, the forts, begun, unfinish'd stand:
The mighty structure threat'ning from on high
120 Hangs interrupted—all inactive lie
Unbrac'd,—the vast machines that thro' the air,
Lab'ring, the pond'rous mass, aloft, suspended bear.
When Juno view'd the tumult in her breast,
That Fame with Passion could no more contest,
She sought the Cyprian queen, «What praise, what fame»
126 She cried, «what glorious triumph you may claim,
What high renown, for you and for your son!

Two mighty gods—one woman have undone!
I'm not deceiv'd, I know what jealous hate
130 Our rising walls and Punic pow'r create;
To what extreme, what purpose will it tend?
Why may not peace and nuptial union end
This dire debate?——You've gain'd your utmost aim;
Thro' every fibre Dido feels the flame;
135 She doats, she burns;—then let the nuptial rite,
At once the people, and the chiefs, unite,
And both the nations be alike our care;
The sceptre let the Phrygian husband bear,
And take my Tyrians for the nuptial dow'r».
140 Venus who saw how much the Latian pow'r;
The promised empire in the Trojan line
Alarm'd the goddess, felt her false design,
But smiling said, «Who madly would refuse
Such offers—and eternal warfare choose?
145 Would Fortune friendly on our project wait.
But doubts within my mind arise, if Fate
And Jove allow, that, with the sons of Troy,
The Tyrian race one empire should enjoy,
The people mingled, and their rites combin'd.
150 'Tis yours; his queen, to try the thund'rer's mind;
Mine to obey»—«Be that my care,» replied
Jove's sister Queen—«Now hear what I provide:
To-morrow, when the rising lamp of day
Shoots o'er the humid orb its golden ray,
155 Unhappy Dido and her guest of Troy
Together in the woods the chase enjoy,
When ev'ry mind is on the sport intent,
From gather'd clouds with livid light'ning rent,
Of rain and pelting hail, a horrid show'r,
160 With peals of thunder on their heads I'll poor:
All fly the storm, and in one dark retreat,
The Trojan hero, and the Queen shall meet;
There will I be; there if unchang'd your mind,
Shall Hymen's chain at once the lovers bind».
165 The Queen of love perceiv'd her false intent,
Smil'd at the smooth deceit, and bow'd assent.
Aurora now her wat'ry couch forsakes,
The chosen youth her earliest beam awakes,
The bounding steed, the highly scented hound,
170 Nets, toils, and spears, the palace court surround.
A favour'd band within the royal gate,

The Queen who still delay'd, respectful wait.
In purple trapping, burnish'd gold array'd,
Proud on the foaming bit, her courser play'd;
175 She comes; the court her graceful steps surround;
Her Tyrian vest, embroider'd fringes bound;
Her quiver gold, with gold her hair enlac'd,
A golden clasp her flowing mantle brac'd.
Next with his Phrygian youth Iulus came
180 On wings of joy; but charms divine proclaim
Cythereas offspring as he join'd the train.
Thus when young Phoebus leaves the wintry plain,
From Lycia and the Xanthian flood, retires
To native Delos, and his sacred choirs;
185 Mingled in carols loud around his shrine,
Cretans and Greeks, and painted Scythians join.
Graceful on high the god o'er Cynthio glides,
His wanton locks with pliant gold divides,
With tender foliage crowns his radiant hair;
190 Wide sounds the dart bu spreading shoulders bear.
Æneas moves not with inferior grace,
Such heav'nly beauty beam'd upon his face.
O'er hills and rocks, and thro' the pathless wood,
From their old haunts they rouse the savage brood;
195 Here downward springs the shaggy goat, and here,
From the steep cliff down rush the bounding deep,
Dart from the hills, in panting herds unite,
Stretch o'er the plain and spread their dusty flight.
As thro' the vale Iulus winds his steed,
200 Leads on the chase, and passes all in speed,
A nobler prey his youthful vows implore,
The tawny lion or the foaming boar.
But murky clouds are gath'ring round the pole-,
In hollow murmur distant thunders roll;
205 The hail, the rain a mingled tempest pour,
Whole rivers swelling down the mountain roar,
The trembling youths of Troy, the Tyrian train,
Cytherea's grandson, scatter'd o'er the plain,
All fly the storm, and in one dark retreat
210 The Tyrian Queen and Trojan Hero meet.
Strait nuptial Juno, gives the fatal sign;
Pale flames the torch, and trembling Earth the shrine:
Night spread the veil;—and to the vow they swore
The murmuring air, ill omen'd witness bore.
215 The frighted Nymphs along the mountain height,

In doleful cries proclaim the genial rite.
That hour her death and all her sorrows wrought;
Then fame and honor vanish'd from her thought;
No more she struggles with a secret flame,
220 The crime is veil'd in wedlock's specious name.
Soon thro' the Lybian towns, Fame blew the deed;
Fame, that outstrips all other ills in speed,
That feeds on motion, strengthens as she flies,
225 Weak, timid first, but soon of monstrous size,
Her feet on earth, amid the clouds her head.
With Heav'n incens'd, her mother Earth 'tis said,
This sister added to the Giant brood,
With wings, with feet, with dreadful speed endu'd.
Huge horrid monster!——Ev'ry plume she wears
230 A watching eye conceal'd beneath it bears,
And strange to tell—on ev'ry feather hung
A gaping ear—a never ceasing tongue.
Sleep never enter'd yet those glaring eyes;
All night 'twixt earth and heav'n she buzzing flies;
235 All day sits watchful on the turrets height,
Or palace roof, the babbling town to fright.
Falsehood and truth, she spreads with equal real,
To gaping crouds rejoicing to reveal
What is, what was, and what has never been.
240 Æneas fled from Troy;—The Tyrian queen,
Her bed, her sceptre, with an exile shares;
And now forgetful of all other cares,
With shameful passion blindly led astray,
In love and joy they waste the hours away.
245 This, all around Fame glories to diffuse,
And to Iarba next her flight pursues,
To fan the flame that in his bosom glows.
To Jove himself, his birth the monarch owes;
A nymph his mother, by a forc'd embrace;
250 And to the God, the author of his race,
Their lofty domes an hundred temples raise,
An hundred shrines with flames perpetual blaze,
Hung round with wreaths: through all his vast domain,
The soil was rich with blood of victims skin.
255 He, by the dire report, to madness fir'd,
Vents his dark soul by jealous rage inspir'd,
Before the gods, while curling incense blaz'd,
His suppliant hands to Jove almighty rais'd.
«All potent Jove! those eyes that view the Moor

260 From painted coaches full libations pour,
See they not this? Or when thy thunder rolls
Do causeless fears, O Father, shake our souls?
Is there no vengeance in the bolt you poise?
Is all but fancied horror, empty noise?
265 A woman, wand'ring outcast on our shore,
Bargains a petty spot and owns no more,
Accepts a portion of our coast to till,
Ev'n from our pity; from our royal will;
And she—the offer of our hand disdains,
270 And she—Æneas in her court detains!
That Paris, with that woman crew, that wear
Those Phrygian bonnets on their scented hair,
Enjoys the spoil.—while I—thy power proclaim,
Adorn thy shrine, and feed on empty fame».
275 Thus, while he pray'd and bow'd before the shrine:
Th' Almighty hearing, throws his eyes divine
On Lybia's coast; there views the lovelest pair
Forgetting fame and ev'ry nobler care,
And quick commands the herald of the sky.
280 «Go, call the zephyrs, spread your pinnions, fly,
Fly to the Dardan chief who ling'ring waits
Mindless in Carthage of the promis'd fates;
Swift as the rushing wind, my order bear.
Not such a man—unworthy of her care,
285 His mother promis'd, when her powerful charms,
Twice, made me save him from the Grecian arms.
No—For Hesperia's realm a future king,
Thro' whom, from Teucer's blood untam'd to spring
A warlike race, the pregnant seeds to lay,
290 Of boundless empire, universal sway.
If he, unmov'd, such' proferr'd greatness sees,
Renouncing glory for ignoble ease.
} Julus too, must he forego his claim?
} Spoil'd by a father of his birthright fame,
295 } The pow'r, the glory, of the Roman name.
What mean these structures in a hostile place?
What hopes deceitful from his mind efface
Th' Ausonian offspring, the Lavinian land?
But let him sail—no more—bear my command».
300 Jove spoke—His son obey'd:—and to his feet
Bound the light wings of gold—wings ever fleet,
Which over earth and sea, through yielding air,
Swift as the wind the rapid herald bear;

305 And took the rod that calls the trembling ghost
To light, or binds it to the Stygian coast,
Gives balmy slumber, breaks the sweet repose,
Weighs down the lid of dying eyes that close.
Thro' storms and dripping clouds with this he glides;
Now o'er the summit and the hoary sides
310 Of Atlas hangs, pois'd on whose shoulders rest
The Heav'ns: his head eternal storms infest,
Crown'd with dark pines, inwrap'd with gloomy clouds;
Primeval snow his shaggy bosom shrouds,
Furrow'd with streams that down his chin descend,
315 And chains of ice from his broad beard that pend.
Here light the God—Balanc'd his equal wings,
And darting forward to the ocean flings.
Through misty air as nearer earth he drew,
Cutting the winds and whirling sands, he flew
320 Like birds, that hov'ring o'er the fishy main,
Drop from the sky', and skim the watry plain.
So from the height his mighty grandsire props,
Down on the pinion light Cyllenius drops;
And scarce his winged feet had touch'd the ground,
325 Æneas with the busy crew he found,
Planning new structures for the rising town.
Bright with a radiant gem his sword hung down,
A mantle graceful o'er his shoulder thrown
With sparkling gold and Tyrian purple shone.
330 'Twas Dido's present: thro' the blushing thread
The docile gold her taper fingers led.
The god accosts him.—«With uxorious care
The walls of Carthage does Æneas rear,
Himself forgotten and his future state?
335 But he that reigns—the pow'r who next to Fate,
Roles Earth and Heav'n, and moves them with a nod,
Thro' skies unclouded, he—the ruling God,
This to your ear commands me to convey;
Why on the Lybian shore this fond delay?
340 These rising tow'rs—If satisfied with these,
You barter glory for ignoble ease,
Your injur'd heir—your young Ascanius view,
Rome and th' Italian reign to him are due.»
While thus the God convey'd what Jove resolv'd,
345 From human eyes in air his form dissolved.
Æneas stood with sacred terror chill'd;
His hair erect, his lips with horror seal'd;

Aw'd by the present God, the high command,
He burns to fly, and leave the much lov'd land.
350 But how alas!—What words, what soothing art?
How meet the Queen, the sad design impart?
Now here, now there, his wav'ring soul inclin'd;
He bends on ev'ry side his anxious mind:
And thus at length his doubting councils end.
355 He bids Cleanthus and the chiefs attend,
The crews assemble and the ships prepare,
In silence hid the object of their care;
While Dido yet the faithless dream deludes,
And not one doubt upon her bliss intrudes:
360 That he, mean while, the fittest time would seek,
The fittest place the sad reverse to speak.
In secret they, the pleasing task pursue;
But soon—(what can escape a lovers view)
Soon Dido saw the change, her boding mind
365 Fancied, foresaw, or felt what they desgn'd.
Trembling, alive to all she sees or hears,
Suspecting ev'ry thing, she doubts, she fears,
While Fame that wounded feeling never spar'd,
The crews on board announced, the fleet prepar'd:
379 Till mad'ning flames within her bosom rise;
Distracted, furious, o'er the town she flies,
Wild as the Woodnymph when the frantic rite
And Bacchanalian shout, to rage excite
Madder and louder as the God invades,
375 She hears him bounding thro' the midnight shades.
Dido, herself, at length, Æneas sought;
Could you, false man, conceive the cruel thought,
To hide a crime so great—unseen to go,—
Silent, unnotic'd—Would you leave me so?
380 Has love no charm, has plighted faith no tie?
Nor Dido doom'd a cruel death to dye.
And for yourself—unfeeling!—when die skies
With tempest low'r—when wintry blasts arise,
You tempt the dang'rous ocean—to explore
385 A distant, strange, unhospitable shore.
Had Troy herself existed, who would brave
For Troy herself, the treach'rous wintry wave.
'Tis me you fly—Oh, by your sacred vow,
By these sad tears, (they're all that's left me now
390 To move your heart); by all our solemn ties,
By what I've suffer'd, by our shortliv'd joys,

If gratitude has giv'n me any right,
If any charm in me once gave delight,
Do not desert the wreck yourself have made,
395 Nor from my falling state withdraw your aid.
If yet there's any pow'r in pray'rs like mine,
Oh pity me; recal that sad design—
See Africa pow'rs, my feeble realm pursue,
My Tyrians hearts are gone,—'Tis all for you,
400 To you I've sacrific'd my brightest claim,
My sacred honor—all my former fame:
Since the dear name of husband is forgot,
Think, cruel guest, of wretched Dido's lot.
What prospect in her ruin'd state remains?
405 Pygmalions vengeance—proud Iarba's chains.
Of you—of all that's dear in life bereft,
Oh were some pledge of mutual passion left:
Some young Æneas, in whose face alone
His father's dear resemblance I might own,
410 With infant grace my lonely court to cheer,
Not lost, not widow'd quite I should appear».
She ceas'd.—With eyes unmov'd,—o'er aw'd by Jove
He stood, and with contending passions strove.
At length he spoke. «For ever I confess
415 I owe you all that words could e'er express,
And in this grateful heart Eliza reigns,
While life itself, and memory remains.
Ne'er did I hope my voyage to conceal;
Never, (my words are few for all I feel),
420 Be not deceiv'd, no, never did I join
These nuptial ties, nor this alliance sign.
Had Fate, alas, allow'd me to dispose,
To end these troubles in the way I chose,
The ruins of my friends, the wreck of Troy,
425 Should all my care, and all my hope employ.
Then, sailing back to Asia's fertile shore,
For them, should Priam's city rise once more.
But now 'tis Italy Apollo shows,
'Tis Italy the Lycian fates propose,
430 My country's there, there all cry vows unite.
Far from your native soil, if you delight
In Afric's coast, these walls if you enjoy;
Allow Ansonia to the sons of Troy.
We too, in foreign lands a state may raise.
435 As oft as Night her humid veil displays,

Oft as the stars, in solemn glory rise,
My father's murm'ring ghost before my eyes
Brings young Ascanius, and upbraiding stands,
And claims th' Hesperian crown, the promised lands;
440 And even now—(on both their heads I swear)
From Joves high throne above, thro' flitting air,
} The thund'rer's will, the herald God declar'd;
} These eyes beheld him, and these ears have heard;
} He past these walls, and in broad day appear'd.
445 Then cease the wounding accent of complaint—
I follow not my will, but Heav'n's constraint».
She heard his words—but turning from his view,
Now here, now there, her eyes indignant threw.
She fix'd him with a scornful silent cast,
450 All over view'd him—and burst forth at last.
«No, faithless monster, no! Nor race divine,
Nor Dardan sire, nor Goddess mother thine!
Form'd in the flinty womb of rocks accurst,
455 Begot by Caucasus, by tygers nurst.
What need I more? why doubt of what is plain?
One sigh, one look, did all my tears obtain.
How name his crimes? did loves extremest woe,
Move that hard heart, or cause one tear to flow!
But will Jove's Queen who guards the nuptial vow,
460 Will mighty Jove himself, such deeds allow?
Whom now confide in? Cast upon my shore,
Shipwreck'd, distress'd, a friendly aid I bore:
Himself, his fleet, his friends, from ruin drew,
Nay, foolish woman! shar'd my kingdom too,
465 Now,—my rage to very madness tends:
Now Lycian fates, now Phæbus he pretends,
} Nay mighty Jove himself, thro' flitting air
} Sends down a god his dread command to bear.
} A worthy object, truly, for his care!
470 A mighty thing, to break the God's repose!
But go, such fates no longer I oppose;
Go, seek Ausonia in the hollow wind,
And in the frothy surge a kingdom find.
Yes may you find—just Heav'n my wishes serve!
475 Dash'd on some rock, the fate that you deserve.
Then, when you call on injure! Dido's name,
I'll follow glaring in the light'ning's flame;
When Death's cold hand this wretched soul shall free,
My ghost shall haunt you, wheresoe'er you be.

480 Yes wretch—be sure—the vengeance will be paid.
'Twill reach my ear—'twill sooth my angry shade».
While yet she spoke, she trembling turn'd away,
Broke from his sight, and shun'd the light of day.
485 She left him struck with fear, with grief opprest;
Opposing thoughts revolv'd within his breast.
Her languid step her maids supporting led,
And plac'd her fainting on the nuptial bed.
Much as he wish'd the mourner to console,
To speak soft comfort to her wounded soul,
490 To grief, to doubt, to pow'rful love a prey,
Jove's sov'reign will, the hero must obey,
He views the fleet, his brave companions cheers,
Hauls down the bark and to the ocean veers;
The sides well calk'd, the briny wave defy,
495 The living woods, their shapeless limbs supply,
From the green oar the bleeding leaf they tear,
They run, they toil, they press the phasing care.
In gath'ring numbers from the town they pour,
Wind o'er the plain, and spread along the shore
500 Like ants, that forage for a future day, 500
And to their stores the plunder'd wheat convey;
In narrow columns move the sable train;
These with main strength roll on the pond'rous grain;
These press the march, and these the loit'rers drive;
505 They go, they come, their path seems all alive.
Ill fated Queen! what pangs your bosom tore,
What sighs you heav'd, as on the moving shore,
The busy crews, assembling in your sight,
With dashing waves, their horrid shouts unite.
510 Love, in our heart! how boundless is thy force!
To tears again, to pray'r she has recourse;
Love bends her soul each suppliant art to try,
Each humble suit, ere she resolve, to die.
«See, Anna, see, the crowded beach they hide,
515 See how they spread, they swarm from ev'ry side;
Their open sails already court the wind,
The stern with wreaths the joyful sailors bind.
Oh had I thought such ills could e'er ensue
Perhaps I should have learn'd to bear them too?
520 Now grant me, Anna, grant this one request!
False man! his friendship you alone possest;
To you his heart was open, none but you,
The soft access, the pliant moment knew.

Go sister then, my haughty foe intreat,
525 Tell him to Troy I sent no hostile fleet;
Nor yet, at Aulis, was I one that swore,
United vengeance to the Dardan shore.
Have I disturb'd his father's sacred shade,
That to be heard—not mere—in vain I've pray'd?
530 Tho' clos'd his ears to me, can be deny
This last, this least request! where would he fly?
Bid him remain till wintry storms subside,
Till kinder breezes, smooth the ruffled tide.
535 The nuptial vow, which he so vainly swore,
His plighted faith no longer I implore,
Nor yet his Latian kingdom to forego:
Some fruitless space, some breathing time for woe,
'Till fate have thought the wretch subdu'd to grieve,
Is all I beg—Obtain this last reprieve—
540 For pity gain it,—and the short delay
With all her parting soul, will Dido pay».
So pray'd the Queen, and o'er and o'er again,
Pray'rs, sighs, and tears her sister urg'd in vain;
Unmov'd he stands by tears, by pray'rs by sighs,
545 The fates oppose, the God his ear denies.
Thus from the rock, the patient work of years,
His knotted strength an oak majestic rears,
When Alpine storms on ev'ry side contend,
Now here, now there his rooted mass to bend,
550 Each labour'd limb resounds, and from his head
The rustling spoils in heaps the ground o'erspread.
He grasps the rock unmov'd, and proudly shoots
As high to heav'n his head, as down to hell his roots.
With storms as fierce the lab'ring Hero torn,
555 Now here now there by swelling passion borne
Sunk in his soul a mighty load of woe,
His mind unshook—tears unavailing flow.
'Twas then that Dido, sinking with her fate,
In all its horror view'd her wretched state.
560 The light of heav'n grew odious to her sight,
She call'd on Death, and each religions rite
With horrid omens urg'd the dark design:
The milky juice flowed black upon the shrine;
And dire to tell, the sacred wine she bore
565 Fell from the cup in fleaks of clotted gore.
These horrid sighs, to her alone reveal'd,
Ev'n from her sister's friendship she conceal'd.

But more—a temple in the palace stood
With snow-white fleeces hang, with garlands strew'd,
570 Where to her former husband's honor'd shade
Assiduous worship, daily vows she paid:
There, when the night, unroll'd her sable pall
She hears his voice in doleful murmurs call,
While from the roof the fated owl alone
575 In deep complaint prolongs the funeral tone.
Beside, what ills had been foretold before,
Now on her mind, a dread impression bore.
Her aching eyes did broken slumbers close,
Æneas like a vengeful fury rose:
580 Alone—forsaken—distant from her home,
Driv'n o'er the desert—she appears to roam
With sinking steps,—abandoned—left behind,
Thro' burning sands her native Tyre to find.
So mad Pentheus saw two suns arise,
585 Two Thebes appear before his haggard eyes.
So wild Orestes flies his mother's rage,
With snakes, with torches arm'd across the stage,
To 'scape her vengeance whereso'er he goes,
Pale furies meet him and his flight oppose.
590 Now when despair had settled on her mind,
What way to meet the death that she design'd
Fill'd all her thoughts. Her sister she addrest
While treach'rous smiles beguil'd her soul distrest.
«Rejoice, my friend, while I the means impart,
595 To gain his love or drive him from my heart:
A place there is where Æthiopia ends,
And into ocean's lap the sun descends;
Where Atlas on his spreading shoulders bears,
And turns the shining glory of the spheres.
600 Thence comes a priestess, in Massyla rear'd,
Who for the watchful Dragon food prepar'd;
Th' Hesperian temple 'twas her charge to keep,
The drowsy flow'rs in liquid honey steep,
And watch the golden branches on the tree.
605 She, at her will, the lab'ring mind can free,
With mystic verse,—or deadly cares enforce,
Repell the stars—arrest the rivers course;
Raise the dead shade, the trembling mountain rend,
And make the wood with horrid sound descend.
610 By heav'n and thee, thou nearest to my heart,
Against my will I fly to magic art.

But in the inmost court, in open air,
A lofty pile thou, dearest friend, prepare,
There let his arms, my nuptial couch that grac'd,
615 There ev'ry thing he faithless left be plac'd;
And fast that bed—sad witness of my fall;
The priestess orders to destroy them all.
Of the sad deed be left no conscious trace—»
She ceas'd and smil'd,—but death was in her face.
620 Anna obey'd; prepar'd the pyre; her mind
Conceiv'd no fear of all the Queen design'd,
Nor with such deep despair, her spirit fraught,
Nor worse than when Sicheus fell she thought.
In open air, but in a court inclos'd,
625 Rich pine and cloven oak the pyre compos'd;
The Queen herself the lofty sides around,
With flow'rs of death, funereal fillets bound;
Then o'er the pyre, upon the nuptial bed,
His sword, his portrait, all he left, she spread;
630 Her spirit labour'd with the dread design;
All round were altars rais'd for rites divine.
There stands the priestess with dishevell'd hair;
(Her voice like thunder shakes the trembling air)
Thrice on the hundred gods aloud she calls,
635 Deep night and chaos, thrice her Voice appalls;
The triple form that Virgin Dian wears,
Infernal Hecate's threefold nature hears.
For stygian waters that surround the dead,
Enchanted juice, a baleful vapour shed.
640 Black drops of venom—potent herbs she steep'd,
With brazen scythes, by trembling Moonlight reap'd.
And from the filly's infant forehead shorn
A powerful philter from the mother torn.
The Queen her sacred off'ring in her hands,
645 With one foot bar'd, before the altar stands;
Her zone unbound releas'd her flowing vest;
The conscious gods her dying words attest,
The start that bear our fate, and if above
A pow'r remains, that pities injur'd love.
650 'Twas night when o'er the earth in soft repose,
All that exist, the load of life depose;
When woods are hush'd, and murmuring billows done,
When stars descending half their course have run;
In silence all—The beasts, the feather'd brood,
655 That swim the lake, or haunt the thicket wood,

All thro' the silent night, in balmy sleep
Their hearts reliev'd in sweet oblivion steep.
Not wretched Dido—night descends in vain
Her eyes unclos'd, and unrepriev'd her pain;
660 Rest flies her soul, and sleep her couch forsakes;
Care through the livelong night incessant wakes;
Now love, now rage, in midnight silence nurst,
Back on her soal with doubted fury burst.
From wave to wave of boiling passion borne,
665 «What now remains, she cries—despis'd, forlorn,
Must Dido now, poor suppliant wretch, implore,
And court the husband she disdain'd before;
Or must I on their fleet submissive wait;
And from those Dardan lords expect my fate?
670 Oh! yes!—by former favours I may guess
What gratitude they'll feel in my distress.
But if—which way! what means?—What pow'r have I?
How will their pride my humble suit deny?
Oh senseless being! have I yet to know,
675 How far, that perjur'd, Trojan race can go?
And then—alone attend their joyful crew,
Or with my Tyrian force their fleet pursue?
Yes,—and the men I scarce from home could tear,
680 Will they for me again the ocean dare.
No—meet the death you merit.—Let the sword—
'Tis all that's left, this sad relief afford.
Oh, sister, to my tears so weakly kind,
You nurst this fatal error in my mind,
} You wrought my fate, you gave me to my foe;
685 } As Nature free, unshar'd my days might flow,
} No guilty joy, no faithless partner know,
No pangs like these I bear,—and not to you,
Dear injur'd shade, Sicheus not untrue».
Long as the gloomy shades o'erhung the pole,
690 Such cares revolving prey'd upon her soul.
Meanwhile Æneas in his fleet repos'd,
His doubts remov'd, and all for flight dispos'd.
To him the form divine he'd seen before,
Appear'd in sleep—again his mandate bore;
695 The graceful limbs of youth, the flaxen hair,
The voice, the rosy hue, Jove's son declare.
«O goddess born! can sleep weigh down your eyes,
Clos'd to the dangers which around you vise?
Senseless!—the zephyrs waste their fav'ring breath,

700 While brooding in a soul resolv'd on death
Some black design, matures, some treach'rous blow,
Haste then and fly, while yet you've pow'r to go.
You'll see, if here you wait the morning ray,
The port block'd up, the shore to flames a prey.
705 Woman's a thing so variable and light!
Haste then away. He spoke and mix'd with night.
Æneas trembling as the phantom flew,
Started from sleep, and rous'd the slumb'ring crew.
«Rise, rise, companions, each one to his oar;
710 Hoist ev'ry sail—a god sent down once more,
Impels our flight—Be quick—stand out to sea,
The cables cut. Great God, whoe'er you be
Thy words again exulting we obey.
Be present, rule our stars—direct our way
715 Propitious». He spoke, his whirling falchion drew,
The halser cut, the bark impatient flew,
All felt the impulse—dashing thro' the tide
They quit the shore, their barks the ocean hide;
The boiling wave their oars alternate sweep,
720 They bend, they pull, they cut the sounding deep.
Now rising from Tithonius golden bed
Fresh beams of rosy light Aurora shed;
And as the scatter'd shades were pierc'd with grey,
The Queen from high beheld them under way,
725 Their swelling sail the fav'ring breezes bent,
The shore, the port, a lonely space present.
Oh then her lovely bosom in despair
She beat. Oh then she tore her flaxen hair.
«He's gone—Almighty heav'n, he's gone! she cries,
730 That wand'ring exile all my pow'r defies.
Arm, arm, my warriors—sally from the town;
Pursue the wretches—haul my gallies down;
Bring flaming brands, with sails with oars pursue.
—What have I said, alas! what would I do?
735 Where am I—and my mind what phrenzy leads!
Now Dido, now, you feel your impious deeds.
Then was the time, your sceptre when you shar'd.
O thou for faith, for piety rever'd!
This, this is he whose pious shoulders bore
740 His gods, his father, from the Trojan shore!
Why did I not those limbs to pieces tear,
Behold the waves, the bloody fragments bear,
Cut off his friends and sever'd with the sword,

Serve up Ascanius at his father's board!
745 His fortune might prevail—and so it might!
What has despair to fear—in Fortune's spite
I'd fire the fleet, the town, the son, the sire,
The race extinguish, and with joy expire.
«O Sun, whose beams all earthy deeds reveal,
750 Juno who know and witness what I feel,
Hecate whose howl the midnight hour affrights,
Gods of my parting soul—avenging sprites,
Accept my vow, my pray'r expiring hear;
The ills I bear are worthy of your ear».
755 «If so the fates decree, if Jove command,
That, he accurst, shall reach th' Italian land,
There may he meet in arms, a warlike race,
There helpless rove, torn from his son's embrace,
His friends untimely end there let him feel;
760 For succour there to strangers meanly kneel;
And when for peace, ingloriously he sues,
His crown, his life, untimely may he lose,
And lie unburied on the naked shore;
765 With the last breath of life this pray'r I pour.
And you, my Tyrian friends—thro' times extent
On that curst race eternal hatred vent.
These gifts, these honors, let my ashes reap,
No peace, no treaty with that people keep.
770 Rise, rise some vast avenger from my tomb,
With fire with sword that Dardan breed consume.
Now and as long as Fate the pow'r shall lend,
May shore with shore—may wave with wave contend,
So prays my soul—let arms with arms engage,
And children's children war eternal wage.
775 So Dido pray'd, while her distracted thought
To shun light's hated beams, impatient sought.
To Barce then, her husband's nurse, she said,
(Her own at Tyre, within the tomb was laid).
Go, Barce, go my sister hither bring
780 With water sprinkled from the sacred spring;
Bid her the victims lead, the rites prepare,
And you yourself a sacred fillet wear:
The rite began to Stygian Jove we'll end,
My cares shall vanish as the flames ascend,
785 His image wasting as the pyre consumes»;
She spoke—the step of age officious haste assumes.

But now the ripen'd project chill'd her soul;
Thro' starting blood her eyeballs burning roll;
Her cheek convuls'd with spots of livid red,
790 All pale and ghastly, Death approaching spread.
Strait to the court with darting stop she bends,
With frantic haste the funeral pyle ascends,
And from the scabbard draws the Dardan blade.
(Sad gift, alas, for no such purpose made),
795 But when the bed, and Trojan vest she view'd;
That well known bed—she paus'd—and pensive stood.
Tears found their way—once more that bed she prest
As these last words her parting breath exprest.
«Dear pledges! yes!—while heaven allow'd it so?
800 Now take this soul—-relieve me from this woe;
I've liv'd, whatever fortune gave is o'er;
No common shade I seek the dreary shore,
My walls arise, I leave a glorious state;
—Not unreveng'd I view'd my husband's fate;
805 Alas, too happy—had the envious gales,
To Lybia's coast, ne'er bent the Phrygian sails».
She ceas'd—and kiss'd again the fatal bed:
«—And must I die—and none avenge me dead?
Yes, yes! I die, since fate will have it so,
Thus, even thus, well pleas'd beneath the shades I go;
810 These rising flames his cruel eye shall meet,
A dreadful omen to attend his fleet»!
With this they saw her falling on the sword;
Her blood along the reeking weapon pour'd,
815 Ran trickling down her hands.—Now horrid cries
Through all the palace all the town arise—
Fame blows the deed—loud shouts from heav'n rebound,
And groans and yells and female shrieks resound,
As loud and shrill as if to foes a prey,
820 Carthage or ancient Tyre abandon'd lay,
And thro' the temples and abodes of man,
Fierce flames with undistinguish'd fury ran.
Her sister hears the tumult of despair,
She starts—she tears her breast, she reads her hair,
825 And wildly bursting thro' the gathering crowd,
Calls on her dying sister's name aloud:
Dido—Dear sister—how am I betray'd!
For this, these flames—this pyre, these shrines I made.
Oh what complaints for me forlorn suffice!
850 Could you, resolv'd to die, your friend despise,

Was I unworthy deem'd to share your end?
One pang our souls should free, one fate attend.
I call'd our gods—my hands these rites prepar'd;
You go without me, and our fate unshar'd?
835 Oh, sister! this sad deed has ruin'd all;
With you, your state, your friends, your sister fall.
—But pour the stream—I'll wash the blood away,
And if some ling'ring breath of life delay,
These lips shall catch it.—On the pyre she prest
840 Her sister, just expiring, to her breast;
She wip'd the blood—and Dido heard her cries,
And strove to raise in rain her languid eyes,
They clos'd again,—and babbling in the wound
The frothy blood hiss'd forth a horrid sound.
845 Thrice on her hand she lean'd to raise her head,
And thrice sank down unable on her bed;
Her eyes half fix'd, she open'd to the day,
And groan'd that stil they felt the vivid ray.
Till Juno who beheld her ling'ring death,
850 The painful agony of parting breath,
Sent Iris down in pity from the sky,
To free her soul, and loose the stubborn tye.
For since unclaim'd by Fate, before her day,
She fell to love forlorn a guiltless prey,
855 } To cut the tress, the queen of night delay'd,
} The flaxen hair that on her forehead stray'd,
} Nor yet consign'd her to the Stygian shade.
Then Iris, going from the sunbeam drew
A thousand colours, varying as she flew;
860 Her dewy wing in liquid azure spread,
Dropt down the sky, and hov'ring o'er her head
«Pluto, this fated lock I bear to thee,
And from this body set the spirit free»,
She said—Her fingers cut the flaxen hair,
865 The heat dissolv'd—the soul exhal'd in air.

* * * * *

THE HENRIAD.
CANTO IX.
ARGUMENT.

Description of the Palace of Love.—Discord implores his aid to bend the unconquerable courage of Henry IV.—Description of Gabrielle d'Etree. Henry, passionately enamoured with her; quits his army, and loses the advantages of his victory at Ivry. Mornay seeks him in his retreat, tears him from the arms of his mistress, and restores him to his army.

WHERE fam'd Idalia's happy plains extend,
As Europe's bounds begin and Asia's end,
Stands an old palace, long by time rever'd;
The first rude plan the hand of nature rear'd;
5 But soon, disdaining Nature's simple taste,
Intruding art the modest fabric grac'd.
There vernal breezes fann'd the myrtle shade,
Soft odour breath'd, and beams unclouded play'd.
No tyrant winter e'er despoil'd the grove,
10 Bid feather'd warblers end the note of love,
Or bound the murm'ring rill in icy chains.
Eternal verdure crown'd the blissful plains;
No labour Earth requir'd, no season knew,
Unbid by man her smiling harvest grew;
15 Round mellow fruit, the timid blossom twin'd,
Gay Flora's bloom to rich Pomona join'd.
Not wanton Nature when her reign began,
Such blessings lavish'd on her fav'rite man;
The thoughtless joy which from abundance flows,
20 Days without care, and nights of calm repose:
All to delude the mind, to charm the sense,
All Eden e'er could boast,—but innocence.
Sweet music wafted on the balmy breeze,
Invited languor and voluptuous ease,
25 While am'rous lays in dulcet note proclaim
The lovers triumph, and the fair one's shame.
There to the laughing god in flow'rs array'd,
The graceful throng their daily homage paid;
There in his temple learn'd the fatal art,
30 To please, seduce, and captivate the heart.
Young Hope, in flatt'ring smiles for ever gay,
To Love's mysterious altar leads the way:
The graces round, half veil'd and half in sight,
Enticing motion with their voice unite;
35 While Indolence, luxurious laid along,
Listless and loit'ring, hears the tender song.
There, silent Myst'ry, with the veil she wears,
And eyes conversing with the soul, appears,
Attentive tender cares, attracting smiles,
40 Gay sport and mirth, and all that thought beguiles.
Lascivious pleasures group'd with wanton ease;
And soft desires that more than pleasure please.
Such the delightful entrance of the dome:
But onward if with guardless step you roam,

45 And thro' the deep recess audacious pry,
What alter'd scenes of horror strike your eye!
No pleasures form'd in playful groupes invite,
No dulcet sounds the ravish'd ear delight;
50 No tender cares:—- But in their place appear,
Sullen Complaint, and cloy'd Disgust, and Fear;
There, fever'd Jealousy with livid hue,
And falt'ring steps unwinds Suspicion's clew;
Arm'd with the blood-stain'd instruments of death,
There, Rage and Hatred spread their poison'd breath;
55 While Malice, brooding over secret guile,
Repays their labour with a treach'rous smile;
Remorse, that never sleeps, brings up the rear,
Hates his own deed, and drops a barren tear.
There, Love, capricious child, had chose to reign,
60 And pains and pleasures were his motely train;
Cruel and kind by turns, but ever blind,
The dear delight, the torment of mankind,
Thro' ev'ry camp, thro' ev'ry senate glides,
Commands the warrior, o'er the judge presides;
65 Still welcome to the heart, he still deceives,
Pants in each bosom, thro' all nature lives.
High on a throne of endless conquest vain,
Love bids the monarch drag his servile chain;
And glorying less to please, than to destroy,
70 In scenes of woe exults with savage joy.
Him, Discord sought, by Rage relentless led,
The timid pleasures knew the fiend and fled;
Her eyes were fire, fresh blood her forehead dy'd,
Around she whirl'd her flaming torch, and cry'd:
75 «Why sleeps my brother o'er the poison'd dart?
His pow'r forgetting o'er the human heart?
Did ever Love the flames of Discord waft,
Or Discord's venom tinge Love's deadly shaft?
Did I for Love, bid madd'ning worlds engage?
80 Rise then—avenge my insult, serve my rage;
Behold a conqu'ring king my pow'r defy!
Crush'd by his hand, behold my serpents die!
See dove-ey'd Mercy smiling by his side,
Thro' fields of civil rage his faithful guide;
85 See to his standard ev'ry heart return,
While I my falling empire vainly mourn:
Let him, with her, obtain one conquest more,
Paris is his, and Discord's reign is o'er:

Her smiles will gild the triumph which he gains,
90 Then what is left for me but hopeless chains!
But Love shall wind this torrent from its course,
And soil his glories in their limpid sourse;
Spite of the virtues which adorn his mind,
In am'rous chains that haughty spirit bind.
95 Can you forget what heroes once you charm'd,
Whom at her feet fair Omphale disarm'd?
Whose purple sail before Augustus flew,
Who lost the world for Egypt's queen and you?
To these proud trophies Henry's name unite,
100 Beneath your myrtle all his laurels blight:
You serve yourself, when you my throne maintain,
For Lore and Discord must together reign».
So spoke the monster, and the vault around
Trembling, threw back on Earth the deadly sound.
105 Love heard, and answ'ring with a doubtful smile,
Where half was sweetness, half insidious guile,
His golden quiver o'er his shoulder threw,
And gliding soft thro' yielding azure flew.
Pleasure, the graces, and unthinking sport,
110 Born by the Zephyr, were his wanton court.
Pois'd on his even wing, he look'd with joy
On Simois, and the plain where once was Troy;
A smile the triumph of his heart betray'd,
To view the mighty ruin Love had made.
115 On Venice, long were bent his partial eyes,
Thro' the blue main where gilded domes arise:
Old Neptune saw them pierce the curling wave,
Own'd the audacious conquest,—and forgave.
To fam'd Sicilia next his flight he bends,
120 Stoops on the purple pinion, and descends
Where he himself inspir'd the Mantuan swain,
And taught Theocritus his tender strain;
There, Fame reports, by ways unknown, he led
The am'rous stream to Arethusa's bed.
125 Then on the downy sail he sought Vaucluse,
Retreat of Petrarch's love and Petrarch's muse;
Fond Echo yet remember's Laura's name;
And what she gave in love repays in fame.
Eure's winding shores his fond attention draw,
130 Where Love's own work, Anet's proud dome he saw;
The fretted ceiling, Henry's cypher grac'd,
By Love himself with fair Diana's plac'd.

The graces dropt a crystal tear, and threw
Around her urn fresh roses as they flew.
135 His wing at length on Ivry's plain he clos'd,
Where Bourbon's thunder for a lime repos'd;
But while the native of the wood he chas'd,
The manly sport war's dreadful image trac'd.
Love spread his chains, and sharp'ning ev'ry dart,
140 Inhuman pleasure bounded in his heart.
«Arise ye winds,» he cried, «the storm prepare,
Collect the pregnant clouds, and dim the air;
The hanging torrent from their bosom pour,
Bid forked lightening fly, and thunders roar».
145 Too soon the blust'ring slaves his will obey'd
Their dusky pinions spread a moving shade;
} O'er the bright scene, dark low'ring mist they drove,
} The languid beam with night usurping strove,
} Pale Nature wept the change and knew the work of Love.
150 Benighted and alone, the king pursu'd
A light that glimmer'd thro' the distant wood:
Love whirl'd his torch, and cast the treach'rous ray,
Like earth-born vapours glitt'ring to betray:
Which lead the trav'ller to the fatal brink,
155 Then leave him to his wretched doom and link.
Fate so decreed it—in this lonely spot,
Retreat and calm, a noble fair one sought;
Far from the tumult of contending arms,
A solitary castle hid her charms,
160 Her tender form from all mankind conceal'd,
While war detain'd her father in the field.
But while his sov'reign's toil the vet'ren shar'd,
His lovely child the fost'ring graces rear'd.
D'Etree (that name the favour'd mortal bore),
165 Of ev'ry, charm exhausted Nature's store.
Not on Eurota's bank, so beauteous shone
The faithless partner of the Spartan throne;
Not she who conquer'd, whom the world obey'd,
On Cydnus when in pomp of charms array'd,
170 Mortals deceiv'd, in awful rapture gaz'd,
And incense to the present goddess blaz'd.
Scarce had she gain'd the charming dang'rous years,
A pow'r too sure, when rising passion bears.
Pure as heav'ns image in the crystal deep,
175 Ere clouds arise, when wanton zephyrs sleep,

Her breast for love and gen'rous feeling form'd,
No sigh had heav'd, no tender passion warm'd.
In vain the treasures of the budding rose,
From am'rous gales their modest folds enclose;
180 As vernal suns each timid charm display,
They yield, and blushing, own the genial ray.
Love, treacherous god, still fertile in deceit,
Long sought the maid, yet seem'd by chance to meet.
A shepherd's boy he came, in outward shew,
185 His back no quiver bore, his hand no bow:
Careless he cried,—but so that she might hear,
«See Ivry's hero thro' our grove appear!
See Henry comes!» The voice of Love conveys
A secret wish to see him, and to please:
190 A conscious blush diffus'd a livelier hue,
Love felt the charm, and glory'd in the view.
Sure of his triumph with such beauty's aid,
Full in the monarch's sight he plac'd the maid.
Around her dress he threw that careless air,
195 It seem'd what Nature's self would choose to wear;
Her auburn locks in easy tresses play'd,
Now hid her snowy neck, and now betray'd;
No muse can paint what playful zephyr show'd,
Nor tell the charm that modesty bestow'd:
200 Not the stiff airs that prudish virtue arm,
The foes of love, the bane of ev'ry charm:
Sweet, bashful grace, that bends the timid eye,
Spreads o'er the glowing cheek a heav'nly dye,
With soft respect extatic rapture blends,
205 And heavn's pure bliss to Love triumphant lends.
But Love does more: for Love what pow'r can bound?
A charm invincible he calls around,
Their tender boughs enchanted myrtles spread,
Rise thro' the earth and wave their taper head:
210 Deluded mortals seek the tempting shades,
The secret charm their languid sense invades,
Around, a stream in lulling manner flows,
Of deep forgetfulness, of soft repose;
Bound in the chain no more they seek to move;
215 Fame, honor, duty, what are you to Love?
Here all alike the sweet delusion share,
And breathe delicious poison with the air.
All whispers love, the birds on ev'ry spray
Prolong the kiss, and swell the am'rous lay;

220 The hardy swain, who with the peep of dawn,
Jocund and careless sought the russet lawn,
Heaves as he goes involuntary sighs;
Unusual troubles in his breast arise,
Beat in his pulse, his loit'ring feet retain;
225 Neglected lye the treasures of the plain:
The same soft charm the trembling maid deceives,
The herd forgot, the sheaf unbound she leaves.
How could d'Etree with such a pow'r contest!
A god invincible her soul possest.
230 In vain, alas! that fatal day she strove,
With youth, with glory, with her heart and love.
In rain a rising voice in Henry's breast,
Back to his ranks the love-lost hero prest;
A pow'r unseen repell'd the gen'rous thought,
235 His virtue vainly in himself he sought;
His soul empassion'd, deaf to honor's call,
Could hear but love, d'Etree possess'd it all.
Meanwhile his chiefs, impatient on the plain,
His absence mourn'd, and sought their king in vain;
240 A thousand dangers for his life appear'd,
For Henry's fame what danger could be fear'd?
No hope of victory the troops inspir'd,
Lost was their ardor when their chief retir'd.
Still the good genius of the realm was near,
245 To cheer their courage, to dispel their fear.
Summon'd by Lewis, from the realm of light
Downward the spirit shap'd his rapid flight,
Around this earthly planet cast his eyes,
To find below a mortal truly wise.
250 Not in the noisy school, or silent cell
Where pray'r, and meagre fast, and study dwell;
Amid the tumult of the martial train,
With rest and conquest flush'd, on Ivry's plain,
Where Calvin's banners to the sky were rear'd,
255 The man he sought, the real sage appear'd:
Mornay was he.—Heav'n form'd the man, to show
That Reason's light may guide us here below;
Plato her voice, and good Aurelius heard,
She led the Pagan right, when Christian's err'd.
260 Such modest candour temper'd manly sense,
When Mornay censur'd, none could take offense;
For truth by him, in winning form convey'd,
Was but the virtue which his life display'd.

Still lean'd his heart the faults of men to bear,
265 While reason told him, all men had their share;
But mid surrounding vices ever pure,
Nor ease nor pleasure could his soul allure.
As thro' the bosom of the briny tide,
Thy limpid waters Arethusa glide,
270 And yet unsully'd by the neighb'ring deep,
Unmix'd and pure their spotless tenor keep.

By friendship guided, gen'rous Mornay came
Where loiter'd Henry, mindless of his fame;
275 The artful god prolong'd the am'rous trance,
And in her hero rul'd the fate of France.
No sameness there the varied bliss destroy'd,
No languor chill'd, no forward pleasure cloy'd;
Each wish attain'd, another wish inspires;
280 Each new enjoyment led to new desires:
Such vary'd ways to please, love taught d'Etree,
Nor time nor habit stole one charm away.
The god with anger blushing as he view'd
Mornay and wisdom on his reign intrude:
Turn'd with revengeful instinct to his dart,
285 And aim'd the deadly shaft at Mornay's heart.
His anger and his arms the sage defy'd,
His breast the bounding arrow turn'd aside:
Impatient for the monarch's lonely hour,
He rov'd indignant thro' th' enchanted bow'r.

290 Where silver streams a myrtle grove inclose,
The veil that timid love and mystry chose,
With all her charms d'Etree her lover blest:
Now flames consume, now languor fills his breast;
Soft drops of pleasure glisten'd in their eyes,
295 Voluptuous tear that love knows how to prize;
No coy reserve the burning bliss restrain'd,
Fond passion, prodigal of pleasure, reign'd;
While Love's mute eloquence their lips employ,
Short sighs and gentle murmurs speak their joy:
300 Their panting hearts with glowing transport swell,
Which love alone inspires, alone can tell.

Young pleasures sporting in luxurious ease,
And infant Cupid's on his amour seize;
Some dragg'd the bloody cuirass o'er the ground,
305 Or from his thigh, the pond'rous blade unbound;
Some from the casque the crystal torrent pour'd,
To wash the crimson spot that stain'd the sword,

And laugh as in their feeble hand they wield
The crown's support, the terror of the field.
310 Discord, who view'd him with insulting spite,
In savage accents utter'd fierce delight;
Rous'd up the league, the happy moment prest,
Reviv'd her serpents drooping in her breast;
And while the monarch languished in repose,
315 Blew the shrill blast, that gathered all his foes.
A conscious blush on Henry's forehead glow'd
As Mornay met him in the soft abode:
Silent at first, the mutual look they fear'd,
But in that silence all the mind appear'd:
320 And Mornay's eye to Henry's soul convey'd,
How wide from virtue and from fame he stray'd.
The gentlest touch of blame we scarce endure,
How oft we loose the friend we mean to cure;
But Henry thus:—«My friend, be ever dear,
325 Who speaks of virtue most be welcome here;
Come to my heart, which yet for glory burns;
My fame, my spirit, with my friend returns;
Away the sweets of vile ignoble rest!
The soft delusion which my soul possest!
330 Far be the slave enamour'd of his chains;
The last great conquest o'er myself remains:
Glory beams forth—and love no more shall sway.
The blood of Spain shall wash the stain away».
«There», Mornay cried,« the monarch's voice I own;
335 There spoke the guardian of the Gallic throne:
Love thus subdu'd, adds lustre to your state;
Blest who ne'er feels it,—but who conquers, great».
As Henry's lip pronounc'd the last forewel,
What advers passions in his soul rebel?
340 Full of the beauty he adores and flies,
He blames the tear, yet tears still fill his eyes:
Now Mornay calls, now tender love retains;
He goes, returns, and going still remains:
But when she languish'd in his last embrace,
345 Colour and life forsook her lovely face,
A sudden night obsur'd her radiant eyes:
The God beheld—air echo'd with his cries;
He trembled that the envious shades of night
Should rob his empire of a nymph so bright,
350 And quench for ever 'mid th' unfeeling dead,
The flame those heav'nly eyes were form'd to spread;

He prest the drooping beauty in his arms;
With gentle sound recall'd her faded charms;
Her eyes half open'd, sought her love in vain,
355 His name she sigh'd, and dropp'd their lids again.
To life, to love, the god recall'd the fair,
And bid young Hope repeat the tender pray'r.
But Mornay's soul, nor grief, nor beauty move,
Virtue and glory triumph over love:
360 The vanquish'd God, with sullen shame withdrew,
And far from Anet's domes indignant flew.

FINIS.

Printed in Great Britain
by Amazon